FOR CHICHI, JONAH, AND
PETE THE OCTOPUS. . . . .

This book was made with T, L, and a heap of C from my official window seat at Coffee Temple in Seoul, South Korea.

DIAL BOOKS FOR YOUNG READERS
Published by the Penguin Group • Penguin Group (USA) LLC • 375 Hudson Street • New York, New York 10014

USA / Canada / UK / Ireland / Australia / New Zealand / India / South Africa / China
PENGUIN.COM
A PENGUIN RANDOM HOUSE COMPANY

Library of Congress Cataloging-in-Publication Data
Farrell, Darren, author, illustrator. Thank you, Octopus / story and pictures by Darren Farrell.   pages cm
Summary: Octopus helps his buddy get ready for bed, but in most unusual ways. ISBN 978-0-8037-3438-8 (hardcover)
[1. Bedtime—Fiction. 2. Octopuses—Fiction. 3. Humorous stories.] I. Title. PZ7.F2445Th 2014   [E]—dc23   2013027093

Manufactured in China on acid-free paper
1 3 5 7 9 10 8 6 4 2

Designed by Jennifer Kelly & Darren Farrell • Typography by Darren Farrell
The publisher does not have any control over and does not assume any responsibility for author or third-party websites or their content.